The Beautiful Princess & Her B.F.F.

(another book with no pictures)

by Sam Evans

This is another book
with no pictures.

Do you know
what that means?

That's right.
I have to read
all the words.

Uh oh…

Every single one.

Oh no! But what if this book has super *silly* words?!

No matter *what* those words make me say.

You don't really want me to read this book, do you? Yes? OK. Here it goes!

Once upon a time…

In a land far away…

There lived
a beautiful princess…

Oh, maybe this one
won't be so bad.

And her name was…

BRuNHILDa
Bal MacHeR
GloR BiNDeR
KiN BuM.

What? How do you even say that?! Maybe we can just call her Brunie? What do you think?

She didn't like it when people called her **BRuNiE**.

Oh.

Or **BRuNHilDa**.

Uh oh! You mean I have to say her whole name? Every time?

Yes. Her name was

BRuNHILDa

Bal MacHeR

GloR BiNDeR

KiN BuM...

and she wanted the whole wide world to know it.

So every day, whenever she met someone new, she would **SiNG a SoNG.**

And this is how it went.

What?! I don't really have to sing, do I?
Really? You want me to sing?

Hello it's so nice
to meet you hum drum,
My name's BRuNHILDa
GloR BiNDeR KiN BuM...

La tree-dee-da-doh
oh fiddle and hum
Hammina jammina
Bumble my thumb

What's your name? Oh-
it sounds so fun,
My name's BRuNHILDa
GloR BiNDeR KiN BuM...

Wow, that's a hard name to say. You don't think this book will get any *sillier*, do you?

Well it just so happens...

BRuNHILDa BaL MacHeR GloR BiNDeR KiN BuM...

was lonely. She didn't have any friends.

Oh, the poor princess!

One day she was walking in the village when she saw a new girl taking her dog for a walk.

So she sang her SoNG.

Again? Do I really have to sing it again?

Hello it's so nice
to meet you hum drum,
My name's BRuNHILDa
GloR BiNDeR KiN BuM...

La **tree-dee-da-doh**
oh **fiddle** and **hum**
Hammina jammina
Bumble my **thumb**

What's your name? Oh-
it sounds so fun,
My name's BRuNHILDa
GloR BiNDeR KiN BuM...

And what do you know?

The new friend
answered **back.**

Not with a song…

But with a **RaP!**

What?! Oh no! I can't rap!!!

"My friends call me
CaRMella G. BoNG.
But that's not my name
They've got it all wrong"

I never knew I could rap like this!
Do you like new my rap voice?

"My Mommy and Daddy
came from over the sea
So really my name is-
CaRMella McGee

"But that's just my first name
The middle one's **longer**-

Uh oh... this can't be good.

"It's...

La Bongaman
Dongafan
Mo Plonkadonk
Bonger.

"And last of all comes-
my last name, **Oh Yes!**

It's a **LOT** longer
than all of the rest.

Eeeek! Oh no!
I don't think I can do this…

"Kwanhansa
Mangoo
Fwap-a-Slap-a-
ZAMBOO
Zap-Kling-Cap-a
JAM-JAM
Praskimpini
HAM-BAM!

"Yo."

Is it over? Oh, please don't ever make me rap again!

BRuNHILDa BaL MacHeR GloR BiNDeR KiN BuM smiled and took her new friend by the hand.

Then she took a deeeep, deeeep breath…

Oh no, oh no, oh no.

I think I'm in big trouble now...

"It's so nice to meet you, CaRMella McGee La Bongaman Dongafan Mo Plonkadonk Bonger Kwanhansa Mangoo Fwap-A-Slap-A-Zamboo Zap-Kling-Cap a JAM-JAM Praskimpini HAM-BAM," said BRuNHILDa Bal MacHeR GloR BiNDeR KiN BuM.

"You have the most beee-a-uuutiful name."

"What is your dog's name?"

"Oh, his name is
    REALLY hard to say."

Then…
CaRMella McALGee
La Bongaman Dongafan
Mo Plonkadonk Bonger
Kwanhansa Mangoo
Fwap-A-Slap-A-Zamboo
Zap-Kling-Cap a JAM-JAM
Praskimpini HAM-BAM
took a big breath and said…

(oh no… do you think it's another really hard name!)

"His name is **DOuG.**"

The two girls smiled, took each other by the hand and skipped off to the castle to play with the **dragon.**

Dragon? She has a pet dragon?!

And from that day on, they were best friends forever!

B.F.F.s

the end.

Now, whatever you do, don't
read the next page...

RAAAAAAAAAAARRR!

Hey, dragon! Don't eat Doug!

Printed in Great Britain
by Amazon